Kent School District #415
12033 SE 256th Street
Kent, WA 98030

The PRINCESS of BORSCHT

LEDA SCHUBERT   ILLUSTRATED BY BONNIE CHRISTENSEN

A NEAL PORTER BOOK   ROARING BROOK PRESS   NEW YORK

Text copyright © 2011 by Leda Schubert
Illustrations copyright © 2011 by Bonnie Christensen
A Neal Porter Book
Published by Roaring Brook Press
Roaring Brook Press is a division of Holtzbrinck Publishing Holdings
Limited Partnership
175 Fifth Avenue, New York, New York 10010
mackids.com

Library of Congress Cataloging-in-Publication Data

Schubert, Leda.
  The Princess of Borscht / Leda Schubert ; illustrated by Bonnie
Christensen. – 1st ed.
    p. cm.
  "A Neal Porter Book."
  Summary: Ruthie's grandmother, who is in the hospital with pneumonia, says she needs
homemade borscht by 5:00 and young Ruthie, with the help of her neighbors, tries to
make some even without the secret recipe.
  ISBN 978-1-59643-515-5
  [1. Cookery–Fiction. 2. Soups–Fiction. 3. Recipes–Fiction. 4. Neighborliness–Fiction.
5. Sick–Fiction. 6. Grandmothers–Fiction.] I. Christensen, Bonnie, ill. II. Title.
  PZ7.S38345Pri 2011
  [E]–dc22
                                                              2010014520

Roaring Brook Press books are available for special promotions and premiums.
For details contact: Director of Special Markets, Holtzbrinck Publishers.

First Edition 2011
Book design by Jennifer Browne
Printed in August 2011 in China by South China Printing Co. Ltd., Dongguan City,
Guangdong Province

10 9 8 7 6 5 4 3 2 1

To three people who can't be beet:
Bob Rosenfeld, Neal Porter,
and Bonnie Christensen —L.S.

For Leda, Queen of Borscht and
much more! (with special thanks
to Rachael Whalen, Emily Herder,
and Kevin Gross) —B.C.

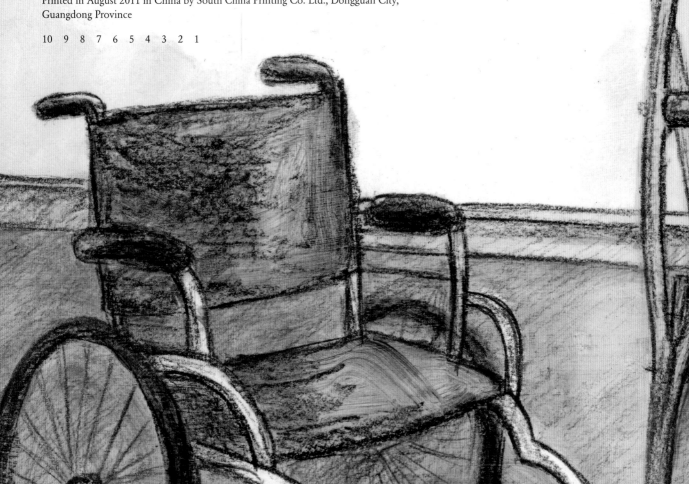

Ruthie peered around the hospital door. Grandma looked tiny in the high, white bed.

"We're here," Ruthie said.

"It's about time," Grandma said. "Give me a smooch."

"How do you feel?" Dad asked.

"I have pneumonia, so how should I feel?" Grandma sounded hoarse. "Besides, a person could starve to death here."

Ruthie was alarmed. "We'll bring you something special."

GET WELL SOON

SPEEDY RECOVERY

Sonia Lorman

Molly Goldberg

ship shape Susan Roser

and Emily

Grandma coughed. "A little homemade borscht, maybe? Then I would get better."

"But I've never made borscht," Ruthie said.

"You should learn," said Grandma. "Your father never has. A tragedy."

"Soup from beets?" Dad said. "Yuck."

"Nonsense," Grandma said. "Everybody loves borscht, especially from my secret recipe." She waved her hand. "Come back by 5:00, or who knows what will happen?"

"Tell me how," Ruthie said quickly. But before they could write anything down, Grandma fell asleep.

At Grandma's apartment, Dad said, "I'll help, but first I need a nap from all the driving."

"It didn't take *that* long to get here," Ruthie said, but Dad was already snoring.

1:30!

Ruthie searched everywhere for the secret recipe.

Then she had an idea and knocked on the door of Grandma's across-the-hall neighbor.

"What a surprise. How's your grandma?" Mrs. Lerman said.

"I have to make her borscht by 5:00 or she'll starve to death. Can you help me?"

"Certainly. I am the Empress of Borscht." Mrs. Lerman pulled on an apron and grabbed a bunch of beets from her counter.

Ruthie found Grandma's soup pot. While the beets cooked, Mrs. Lerman told stories and Ruthie looked for the recipe.

"Okay, done." Mrs. Lerman dropped the beets in ice water. "Now peel," she ordered.

2:30!

Someone knocked on the door. It was Mrs. Rosen from down the hall. "Ruthie, dear, how's your grandma?"

"She needs borscht, and we only have two hours left."

Mrs. Rosen bustled in. "For borscht, I am the First Lady."

Mrs. Lerman frowned. "And I am the Empress."

The First Lady sniffed. "Ha! Ruthie, do you have onions?"

"No onions," said the Empress.

"Does Grandma use them?" Ruthie asked.

The First Lady nodded. "Absolutely." So Ruthie dumped some in the pot. If only she could find the recipe! The simmering soup smelled awful.

"Yoo hoo," a voice warbled from the hall. It was Mrs. Goldberg from next door. "I heard noises. How is your grandma?"

"Starving," Ruthie said. "We're making borscht so she'll get better." "Soup you can't make without me, the Tsarina of Borscht. You have lemons?" The Tsarina squeezed into the kitchen. "Oh, look who's here."

"We're using my recipe," said the Empress.

"Mine," the First Lady said. "With onions."

Ruthie discovered a lemon in the refrigerator and added the juice to the pot.

The Tsarina tasted. "You need sugar for sweetness," she said. "And salt for sour."

"No salt," said the Empress.

"Use honey, not sugar," said the First Lady.
Their voices filled the tiny kitchen.

3:30.

Ruthie yawned. A pinch of salt, two big pinches of sugar.

"We'll go now," said the Tsarina, and the three ladies left, still arguing.

"Thank you," Ruthie said, but nobody heard. She tasted the soup. Something was missing, but there was no one to ask.

She opened Grandma's herb jars. One smelled good, like a pickle, so she threw a pinch into the pot. Then she worried. Soup shouldn't taste like a pickle, should it?

Dad yawned and stretched. "What's happened?" he asked when he saw the mess.

"Just soup," answered Ruthie.

"It looks like borscht," Dad said as he transferred the soup to a thermos. "Yucky."

At 4:30, when they passed the corner store, Mr. Lee waved. "How's the patient?"

"I made her borscht, but maybe it's awful," Ruthie said.

"Ah, your grandma's famous borscht. Almost as delicious as my hot and sour soup," Mr. Lee said, handing her a container of sour cream. "She likes this with her borscht."

Was he the King of Borscht? Everybody in the neighborhood was some kind of royalty.

Grandma was sitting up. "Not a minute to spare," she said. "I was about to eat this awful hospital food."

"Is that why you said 5:00?" Ruthie asked. Grandma nodded, and Ruthie smiled. Grandma wouldn't starve.

"She does exaggerate," Dad told Ruthie. "I thought you knew that." He poured the borscht.

"Your neighbors helped," Ruthie said.

"Pooh. What do they know? For borscht, I am the Queen," Grandma said.

"You know what?" Ruthie said. "You may be the Queen
of Borscht, but I am the Princess."

"Princess Ruthie." Grandma lay back against
the pillows. "You know, tomorrow I
might like a noodle pudding."

Ruthie grabbed a pencil.
"This time we're writing
down the recipe," she said.

She tried the soup. "It's perfect. I bet those ladies never thought of the dill. Only in my recipe."

Ruthie laughed. "And mine! But I didn't find your secret recipe."

"Of course not. It's only in my head." Before Grandma finished the soup, she gave some to Ruthie. Dad wouldn't taste it.

"It's delicious," Ruthie said. "Grandma looks better already."

"Because of my Ruthie," Grandma said, putting down the empty cup.

"You know what?" Ruthie said. "You may be the Queen of Borscht, but I am the Princess."

"Princess Ruthie." Grandma lay back against the pillows. "You know, tomorrow I might like a noodle pudding."

Ruthie grabbed a pencil. "This time we're writing down the recipe," she said.

"Is that why you said 5:00?" Ruthie asked. Grandma nodded, and Ruthie smiled. Grandma wouldn't starve.

"She does exaggerate," Dad told Ruthie. "I thought you knew that." He poured the borscht.

"Your neighbors helped," Ruthie said.

"Pooh. What do they know? For borscht, I am the Queen," Grandma said.

But Grandma was asleep.